Flash Digest

October 2024

Edited by
Terrie Leigh Relf

THE STAFF OF FLASH DIGEST

EDITOR: Terrie Leigh Relf
WEBMASTER: H. David Blalock
COVER DESIGNERS: Laura Givens; Marcia A. Borell

Cover art "The Others" by Amanda Bergloff
Cover design by Laura Givens

Vol. I, No.3   October 2024
Flash Digest is published four times a year on the 1st days of January, April, July, and October in the United States of America by Hiraeth Publishing, P.O. Box 1248, Tularosa, NM, 88352. Copyright 2024 by Hiraeth Publishing. All rights revert to authors and artists upon publication except as noted in selected individual contracts. Nothing may be reproduced in whole or in part without written permission from the authors and artists. Any similarity between places and persons mentioned in the fiction or semi-fiction and real places or persons living or dead is coincidental. Writers and artists guidelines are available online at www.hiraethsffh.com. Guidelines are also available upon request from Hiraeth Publishing, P.O. Box 1248, Tularosa, NM, 88352, if request is accompanied by a self-addressed *10 envelope with a first-class US stamp.

Contents

Stories

10	Chess With a Ghost by Stephen W. Chappell
16	Dead Mall by Paul Lonardo
24	Lovers in the Night-Time by Iseult Murphy
31	Ted by Richard E. Schell
35	The Man in the Chair by Mike Rader
39	Stood Still by Francis W. Alexander
45	Fit for a Queen by Pamela Love

Illustrations

30	Symbiote by Amanda Bergloff
38	Moon Bathing by Iseult Murphy

**THERE'S A SALE GOING ON!!!
IT'S STILL GOING ON!!!**

BUY ALL THE BOOKS YOU WANT AND USE THIS 20% DISCOUNT CODE: BOOKS2024

THIS DISCOUNT CAN BE USED AS MANY TIMES AS YOU WISH, SO TAKE ADVANTAGE OF IT!

GO TO OUR SHOP AT WWW.HIRAETHSFFH.COM

NO MASKS, NO WAITING, AND WE NEVER CLOSE!

A Little Help, Please

In the world of the small indie press we fight a never-ending battle for attention to our work, as writers and in publishing. Here's an example: big publishers [you know who they are] have gobs of $$$ that they can devote to advertising and marketing. Here at Hiraeth Publishing, our advertising budget consists of the deposits for whatever soda bottles and aluminum cans we can find alongside the highways. Anti-littering laws make our task even more difficult . . . ☺

That's where YOU come in. YOU are our best promoter. YOU are the one who can tell others about us. Just send 'em to our website, tell them about our store. That's all. Just that.

Of course, we don't mind if you talk us up. We're pretty good, you know. We have some award-winning and award-nominated writers and artists, plus other voices well-deserving to be heard [not everyone wins awards, right?] but our publications are read-worthy nevertheless.

That number once again is:
www.hiraethsffh.com

Friend us on Facebook at Hiraeth Publishing
Follow us on Twitter at @HiraethPublish1

The Sisterhood of the Blood Moon
By Terrie Leigh Relf

For thousands of Earth years, the Transgalactic Consortium has had an invested interest in this planet and its inhabitants, the Haurans. While the Sisterhood of the Blood Moon and the Guardians work together with the Consortium and Haurans to restore balance to the universe, the Blood Moon is fast approaching. The power of this moon reveals untold secrets . . . including the sacred covenant with the Mora Spiders. There is an ancient pact that continues to be honored - but at what cost and for whose purpose?

The world may come to an end. But will there be a chance for a new beginning? And if so, where?

Type: Novel – science fiction/fantasy
Cover price: $14.95
ISBN: **9781087929927**

Ordering link:
Print Edition:
https://www.hiraethsffh.com/product-page/sisterhood-of-the-blood-moon-by-terrie-leigh-relf

The Saint and the Demon

By t.santitoro & Ron Sparks

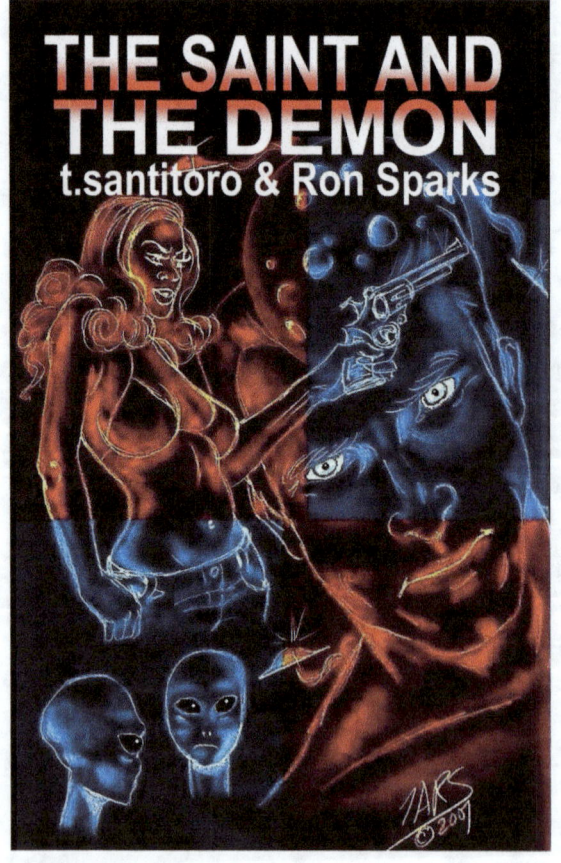

In the not-to-distant future, a young reporter reluctantly agrees to interview a senile old man in the heart of the Florida Everglades. In the humid, swampy environment, the reporter is sure that there can be no story of substance here, but the old man reveals that, in the past, his love was so strong and so passionate for a woman that he stopped at nothing to get her back when the forces of war tore them apart. He became a hero and a coward, a lover and a fighter . . . a saint and a devil. In his quest to rescue the woman he loved, he became something that she could no longer love.

Into the middle of this personal ordeal tumbles Cutter, a man from another world, sent to Earth to establish a breeding mission for his endangered race. He falls in love with an Earth woman, and must defend not only her, but also the future of his own people. The object of his alien affections, an innocent young woman named Angel, finds herself suddenly thrust into a world of aliens and intrigue, and of a love that has far more dangerous consequences than she could possibly have imagined.

Type: Novel – science fiction

Ordering Link:
Print ($13.95): https://www.hiraethsffh.com/product-page/saint-and-the-demon-by-t-santitoro-and-ron-sparks
PDF ($4.99): https://www.hiraethsffh.com/product-page/saint-the-demon-by-t-santitoro-ron-sparks
ePub ($4.99): https://www.hiraethsffh.com/product-page/saint-amp-the-demon-by-t-santitoro-amp-ron-sparks

Chess With a Ghost
Stephen W. Chappell

Roger sat across from the ghost and pondered his next move.

"You gonna make a move, buddy?" the ghost taunted.

Roger looked at the ghost's translucent face and smirked. "Like you got somewhere better to go," he said, moving a pawn.

The ghost sat back, his face twisted in offense. "I've got plenty of places to go," he said haughtily. "Maybe I'll go haunt the bathroom."

"Well, I wish you'd go somewhere. I have a date tonight."

"Huh, right." The ghost pointed to a knight. "Move that one over here."

Roger made a face. "Some ghost you are, can't even move a piece for yourself."

"Oh, I can move a piece all right," the ghost retorted. "I can move all the pieces, just you watch." The ghost spread his arms and stared angrily at the board.

Nothing happened.

"You're not that kind of ghost, Phil," the ghost's wife chided from beside him.

"Ah, come on, Sharon," Phil said. "Always tellin' me what I can do."

Roger rolled back his head and threw out his hands. "Look, can't you two just get a move on already? I've met a lovely woman, and I don't want her running away like the last one."

"She was a tramp," Phil snarked.

"Was not! It hasn't been easy since my divorce, you know. Now go away, you two."

"I don't want to leave," Phil said. Sharon rolled her ghostly eyes.

"Well, it's my place, and I don't want you here anymore."

Phil folded his arms across his chest. "It was my place first."

"Yes, and then you died. I bought it, so it's my place now." Roger moved his knight. "I don't know why I ever started this."

Phil looked delighted. "Because you were lonely, and I was here. I take your knight with that pawn there."

"You sure about that?"

"Yes. I want to take your knight."

Roger shook his head. "Okay." Roger made the move, then took Phil's queen with a rook. "Check."

Phil tried to slam a fist on the table, but it passed through. "Damn it!"

"You're not very good at chess, are you?"

Phil looked at him and contorted his face into a horrible visage: one eye hanging out and bloody worms springing from every opening.

Roger rolled his eyes. "That's terrible. You suck at chess and at being a ghost."

"Well, it's not like they give us a handbook." He pointed at his king and another space on the board, and Roger moved his piece for him.

"Look," Roger said. "If I win this match, then you have to leave. Okay?"

His wife looked at Phil hopefully. "Okay. And if I win, then you have to leave."

"It's my house!"

"Well, then, what do I get if I win?"

Roger thought for a moment. "You can stay in the basement."

Phil shuddered as if chilled. "It's spooky down there."

"Then you should be right at home," Roger smiled and moved another piece.

"Phil," Sharon said, "we do have to be going. We have to move on to the other side, you know."

Phil shot her an angry look. "I'm going to win, and then we won't have to go anywhere." He pointed at the piece he wanted to move.

"How did you all die, anyway? The realtor couldn't say."

Sharon looked sadly at her translucent hands. "COVID. It was the early days, before the vaccine."

"Oh, I'm sorry," Roger said compassionately. "Terrible way to go, that."

"Hey," Phil demanded, "it's your move. One of your last, I'd wager."

Roger smirked. "I bet you're right." He moved his other knight. "Check."

"Argh!" Phil cried. He pointed to his king and where he wanted it moved.

"You're sure?"

"Yes, I'm sure!"

Roger made the move, then moved his queen. "That'd be checkmate." He crossed his arms and smiled. "Now, you two run along. I have to get ready for my date."

"I'm not going," Phil said with a pout. "Nope, I am staying right here and haunting you for all eternity."

"Oh, dear lord," Sharon said.

"Come on, now, we had a deal!" Roger slammed his fist on the table. "She's lovely, and I won't have you ruining our night."

"Oh, getting violent now, are we?" Phil taunted.

"Ha! Don't you just wish you could, you sorry excuse for a ghost!"

Phil slapped at Roger, but his hand passed right through. "Damn it!"

"Come on, Phil, you made a deal. It's time to go." Sharon put her arm around Phil lovingly. "We've been here too long as it is."

Phil sniffled and looked at his wife, the little color he had left draining from his features. "But I'm scared," he admitted.

"I know," Sharon said sadly. "Me, too."

Roger's features softened as he watched them. "Is there anything I can do to help? Burn some incense, maybe?"

Phil shook his head. "No, not that, but thank you." He lifted his head and looked Roger in the eye. "There is something, though. There's a little box I hid in the bathroom. It's behind a loose board under the sink."

Roger left the room and returned a few minutes later with a small jewelry box. "Is this it?"

Phil nodded. "Yes. It was for our anniversary. I never had the chance to give it to her."

Sharon's eyes teared up as Roger held out the box to her.

"You'll have to open it for her, I think," Phil sniffled.

Roger nodded and lifted the lid. Inside was a sparkling ruby heart pendant.

"Oh, Phil, it's beautiful! You shouldn't have." She wrapped her arms around Phil and pulled him close. They glowed brightly in their embrace, and the warmth of their love flooded the room.

Roger watched as they started to fade. Sharon grabbed Phil's face and planted a loving kiss.

"Happy anniversary, my love," Phil whispered as they disappeared, leaving Roger alone.

"So long, you two," Roger said with a tear in his eye as he closed the box. "And happy anniversary."

The Gifted
By Tyree Campbell

DEDICATED TO THE MEMORY OF MELISSA MEAD

The year is 2045. Earth's societies have fallen apart for various reasons—economic, social, political, disease. To live, people began to loot, kill each other, and generally get by from day to day. In the latter stages of this deterioration, fear of disease caused immunizations to be rushed into production without proper testing. Some parents soon discovered that the children born were deformed in some way: flippers for hands and/or feet, missing organs, scales for skin, etc.

In addition to flippered hands and feet, Wendy Meade was gifted with some psi abilities that enabled her to talk with animals and with people. Now an adult woman, she scrapes by in a woods above a bay on the coast of southern Oregon, where there is an abandoned town where food is still available in convenience stores. She supplements this with shellfish from the bay. Such is her life.

Until one day she discovers that she can telepath with animals and people. A small community begins to form around her. Now, if possible, she has to use her powers to protect them from marauders.

Type: Post-Apocalyptic Novel
Ordering links:
Print: https://www.hiraethsffh.com/product-page/gifted-by-tyree-campbell
ePub: https://www.hiraethsffh.com/product-page/gifted-by-tyree-campbell-1
PDF: https://www.hiraethsffh.com/product-page/gifted-by-tyree-campbell-2

Dead Mall
Paul Lonardo

Up until the moment they spotted the old theater, everything had gone as expected, no different than any of the other "dead malls" they'd documented for the two-million-plus subscribers over the past three years.

"Holy shit," Channing howled. "Check out the old movie that was playing when this place closed. What was that, like forty years ago?"

"More like twenty, I think," Aiyden told him.

Anneke slowly panned down from the title on the marquee, SCREAM 3, to the theater doors and walked in behind Channing and Aiyden. The screen at the front was empty, but some of the seats weren't. Aiyden noticed them first and screamed.

Channing did a doubletake. "What the fuck?"

Anneke didn't see the heads until she looked up from her phone. She sucked in a mouthful of air and froze. For a moment, no one spoke, as if anticipating that the people sitting in the total darkness of a theater in a dead mall would suddenly turn around to see where the intrusive light was coming from. But these midnight matinee filmgoers remained perfectly still.

There were about a dozen figures seated up close, and when Channing directed his flashlight toward the back, he revealed two dozen more. The light illuminated their faces, which were shocking and frightful. Their mouths were hinged open in a frozen rictus of laughter, their jaws separated far wider than humanly possible.

"They're mannequins," Channing said and walked up the aisle toward the closest one. It was just a torso that included the head and arms. "Anneke, come closer and get this."

She struggled to keep her hands steady as she filmed them, following Channing from one mannequin to another. They were all wearing various-colored wigs and faded shirts or tank tops. Some of them had no arms.

"It's hard to tell if they're laughing or screaming," Channing said. "So creepy. Who would even make mannequins with expressions like this?"

"Alright, you guys ready to go?" Anneke asked. The truth was that she had seen more than enough already. In the high-intensity brightness of their handheld LED flashlights, it looked to her that Channing and Aiyden were becoming less human the longer they remained inside the three-story wasteland of empty retail stores. She felt like they were all becoming part of the desolate environment.

Before anyone could respond, a shuffling noise in the promenade drew their attention.

"There's someone in here with us." Aiyden whispered.

"Fuck that," Channing shouted. "It's probably a squirrel or something."

"We got everything we need for the episode," Anneke asserted. "Let's just get outta here."

"I'm with Anneke," Aiyden said.

"Hold on," Channing began. "You think there's someone else here, why not get it on film? All we really got right now is just another dead mall with some lame ass mannequins."

"It could be some crazed homeless guy or drug dealers or the cops," Anneke said.

"Whatta you afraid?" Channing goaded, an impish smile giving himself away to her. "Leave the camera on so the subscribers can see you cry, because that's about the only thing that'll make this episode worth watching. Cry. Go ahead. That's all you're good for, anyway. You're a useless, little bitch."

Anneke glared at Channing, trying to play it cool, but she found herself being seduced by his sudden display of sadism. He knew exactly how to push her buttons. Being domineering with her in this situation made her feel even more vulnerable, which only added to her sexual excitement.

Aiyden didn't want to be in the theater with the two of them or the mannequins any longer, and he walked out, willing to take his chances with whatever was out there. The thing that caused him the most anxiety was when Anneke mentioned the potential of police involvement. Being the only one who was over eighteen, he was worried he'd get into serious trouble.

When he noticed someone standing directly behind him, he drew back with a sharp yelp. As soon as he saw the uniform and hat, he started to explain what he and his friends were doing there, but stopped when he realized he was talking to a mannequin dressed as a police officer.

He tapped the mannequin's cheek with an index finger to be sure it was fake. It made a dull sound and he laughed hollowly.

Channing emerged from the theater with Anneke. "I see you made a new friend, Aiyden," he joked.

"This wasn't here when we came in," Aiyden said, panic in his voice.

"Sure, it was," Channing told him.

"I didn't see it, either," Anneke said.

"All right, you didn't see it, but it had to be there."

"I'm done with his place," Aiyden announced, and headed off.

"Me, too," Anneke said, and followed.

"Pussies." Channing punched the mannequin in the face. The fiberglass cop fell to the floor with a thump. "You're both pathetic." He kicked the dummy, sending it scuttling across the floor.

Anneke shut off her phone and stuffed it into her pocket, trading it for a flashlight.

As Channing lagged behind, he started to get a feeling that he was being watched. He stopped to shine his flashlight around but didn't see anything. Suddenly it went out and he was engulfed in total darkness. He heard a shuffling sound behind him and frantically struck the flashlight. It blinked several times before remaining on. Turning quickly, he shined the beam behind him but there was nothing there. He quickly started down the escalator to join his friends. He reached the second floor when he heard movement a floor above. He turned in that direction without the light and saw a shadowy figure at the top of the escalator. He couldn't be sure if it was a mannequin with the face of a demon or the devil himself, but he convinced himself that it was only his imagination.

While walking through the shadowy promenade together, the shuffling sounds intensified, and when they reached the corner of the mall where they had entered through a jagged hole in the masonry an hour earlier, there was now a vacant store.

Anneke gasped and they all froze as the edges of their beams caught images of mannequins occupying the previously empty shops.

"Those definitely weren't here before." Aiyden's voice was weak.

"Someone's fucking with us!" Channing yelled. "I'm going to kill whoever's doing this." He reached into his pocket and withdrew a double-action knife. He slid the switch, releasing the blade.

Hearing a loud sound above, Channing directed his flashlight up to the third floor. Something moved away from the light near the top of the escalator.

"Alright, you fuck, you wanna play games?" Channing charged the escalator and started up, disappearing on the top floor. A moment later, his light was extinguished and he screamed.

Anneke screamed when a human form came tumbling down from the third-floor promenade. She jumped back in horror as a mannequin landed at her feet and exploded, sending limbs and chunks of plaster out in every direction. The decapitated plastic head spun around several times before coming to a rest, faceup, looking eerily like Channing.

"Stay here," Aiyden told her. "Channing's still up there. I'll be right back." He did not sound convincing.

"Don't leave me alone," Anneke pleaded, but she could only watch as Aiyden mounted the frozen escalator and walked up to the third floor. His light grew faint before disappearing completely.

She called out to Aiyden several times, but her throat tightened and when she stepped toward the escalator, her legs stiffened. She strained to get her tight muscles to pull her body up the stairs. Although it was a struggle, she made it to the top floor, where she noticed the mesh-like gate in front of one of the shops was pulled down. Someone wearing an orange jumpsuit was standing just a few feet inside. The mannequin was the exact size and body type as Aiyden. Even the synthetic hair was the same length and style, the hands handcuffed behind its back.

Anneke shook her head, rejecting what she was seeing. In the adjacent store, she caught sight of two oddly positioned mannequins. A naked woman with long, dark hair was laying across the lap of a seated man who was wearing a leather hood over his face and nothing else. The man's right hand was raised, clutching a braided leather flogger with a wood handle. The woman's alabaster butt cheeks were fire engine red. Anneke shined her flashlight directly on the woman's face. The expression on the mannequin was one of complete submission and ecstasy. It was her own face.

Every muscle fiber in Anneke's body grew taut, beginning with her extremities. Her fingers locked and her limbs hardened. With her head and neck fixed, she watched her arm transform into firm, smooth plaster, and then she could no longer move at all. In the next instant, her flashlight went out and she became part of the dead mall forever.

When the Mushrooms Come
The Atomic Age brought with it many wonders and great strides forward. It also brought nuclear war. We often forget how many nuclear warheads are still scattered about our world, and how many countries are still trying to make their own. What would happen to ordinary people if one fell without warning? Follow along in the lives of different people as they move through the drop of a nuclear bomb – before, during, and after the fall. See their lives before the flash, their reactions when the mushroom cloud rises, and how the survivors struggle on.

https://www.hiraethsffh.com/product-page/when-the-mushrooms-come-by-francis-w-alexander

Nefarious & Nightmarish
By Meagan J. Meehan

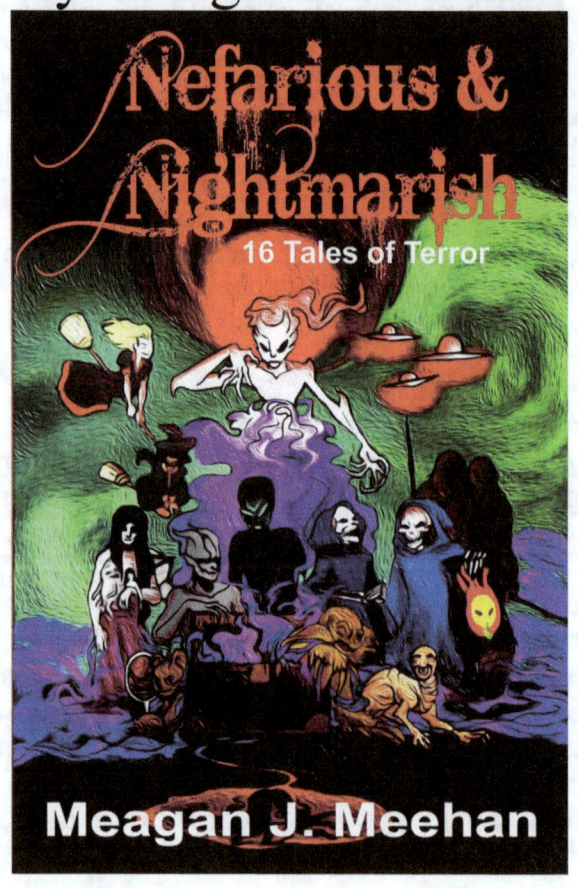

A paranoid truck driver fears aliens but learns that there are even worse things than being abducted; a wealthy bratty girl meets her match when she discovers a genie-like creature in a trunk; two hunters become the prey; a disturbed and sadistic teen learns he isn't the only monster in his community; a security guard has been pursued by the grim reaper since babyhood yet, when it finally catches up to her, she is surprised by its ultimate intentions. These and more encounter strange evils and nightmares. Read this one with all the lights on.

Type: Short story collection – horror

Ordering Link:
Print: https://www.hiraethsffh.com/product-page/nefarious-nightmarish-by-meagan-j-meehan
PDF: https://www.hiraethsffh.com/product-page/nefarious-nightmarish-by-meagan-j-meehan-1
ePub: https://www.hiraethsffh.com/product-page/nefarious-nightmarish-by-meagan-j-meehan-2

Lovers in the Night-Time
Iseult Murphy

The ultimate choice came down to Vlad the vampire or Lupo the werewolf. Belinda stood before them, clutching her single remaining cupid's arrow to her chest.

Murray sat behind the cameras and watched the scene play out on the monitors. It was their last night of shooting. He couldn't wait to get back on a day schedule. He felt like a zombie, although he didn't look anything as shredded as Bob the zombie, who failed to get Belinda's arrow in week one.

He told camera three to pull back to showcase the sweeping staircase of the gothic mansion and the ornate rose window in the long shot. The set designers had really outdone themselves with this one. He made some adjustments to the cameras focused on the reaction shots of Vlad and Lupo and told camera four to move position so that the three contestants lined up better on screen.

"Is Vlad off his mark again?" Murray said.

Casey, the assistant director, looked away from her clipboard and glanced down at the monitor banks.

"Looks like it," she said.

"He's such an ass. Has been all shoot. Where did casting get him from anyway? He's not even that hot."

Casey shrugged. "We're going with the werewolf win first, because they're trending better with audiences, but then we'll reset and film the vampire win."

Murray nodded.

"Ready to roll?"

Casey made the checks, and the call went out to the crew to clear the set.

"Action," Murray said.

At his command, Belinda came to life. Her eyes sparkled as if she was close to tears and her lips trembled with emotion. Murray loved her. She was television gold. She was going to go far.

"Vlad, thank you for letting me into your world. It has been intense getting to know you and understand your lifestyle. I never realised that I was so ignorant about vampires. Thank you for educating me and breaking down my prejudices," Belinda said.

Vlad raised one eyebrow and sneered, showing a glimpse of fang beyond his red lips. Murray sighed.

"The guy is such a hack. How did he make it to the final two?"

"Vampires are sexy," Casey said.

Belinda turned to Lupo.

"Lupo, when we first met, you were like a great big puppy, but I've learned to see the wolf that lies within. Thank you for showing me your vulnerable side. I know transforming three nights a month causes difficulties in maintaining a relationship, but I think we can make it work."

Lupo smiled boyishly and then slightly changed his stance and smouldered to the camera. Murray nodded in appreciation. It was a little cheesy, but the entire show was cheesy. A dating show about a beauty picking her mate from a pack of monsters? How did they even think up these things?

"Lupo, you've transformed my heart from a cat person to a dog lover. Will you accept my final cupid's arrow?"

She held out the cleverly painted wooden prop. Lupo took hold of the golden arrow, grasping the shaft just above Belinda's hand.

"Cut!" Murray roared. "Good work, people. Now set up for the kiss. Make-up, we need touch-ups on the contestants."

A gaggle of crew ran onto the set to change marks and check lighting. Three make-up assistants dutifully trooped up to the contestants, drawing brushes and powders from the bulging tool belts around their waists.

"This stinks," Vlad roared, his voice shaking the set. "I didn't win?"

Murray looked at Casey.

"Did no one fill him in?"

Vlad pulled back his lips, revealing his sharp fangs. He pushed away the throng of crew and grabbed Belinda, one hand tilting her head to expose her long neck, the other sliding around her waist.

"Nice moves. Make a note of that," Murray said.

Belinda seemed to melt in Vlad's arms. Her eyes half closed in ecstasy and she made mewling sounds of pleasure.

"You will be mine." With a scenery chewing snarl, Vlad lowered his head and sank his fangs into Belinda's neck.

Murray sat forward in his chair. "You've got to be kidding me. He's an actual vampire? Like a real undead blood sucking creature of the night?"

Casey leafed through the shooting schedule on her clipboard, as if looking for answers in its marked-up pages. "Eh, I don't know."

"Who cast this guy? This is supposed to be *reality* television. The studio is going to go nuts," Murray said.

On set, Lupo dropped the golden arrow and ran, followed by the make-up assistants. The camera operators stayed in place. Camera three took the initiative and moved in closer to show blood trickling down Belinda's neck as Vlad latched, leechlike, to her vein.

One of the production assistants, Murray couldn't even remember her name, raced screaming onto the set, picked up the abandoned cupid's arrow and drove it into Vlad's chest. The vampire reared back, his clawed hands twitching at the arrow, and then he collapsed into a hideous, desiccated corpse on the plush red carpet.

Belinda sat down with a thump. She looked stoned. The production assistant ran to her and tore off her jacket to apply pressure to the wound.

"Great, now we're down a contestant," Murray said. He threw his hands in the air. "Someone get that person off the lot. She's fired. And get the medics to patch up Belinda. Where's Vlad's stand in? We need him on set in costume in five. Let's reset for the kiss. Oh, someone clean up the mess on the carpet. Come on, people, we can still wrap this up on time."

Murray clapped his hands, and the set became a hive buzzing around him. He rubbed his forehead. Sometimes he regretted giving up alcohol.

Heir Apparent
Tyree Campbell

Answering a distress call, March and Myrrha find a young woman who has deliberately been marooned on an uninhabited world. She claims to be Hoya Palologa, heir to the Palologa throne on Wanderby. But there is already a Hoya who has been invested as the heir apparent to that throne. Myrrha believes the claim of the Hoya she and March have encountered. Thus begins a journey to establish the succession, a journey made far more perilous because Hoya not only claims the throne, but is also a sinister personage with several crimes on her resume.

March and Myrrha find themselves embroiled in internal politics on Wanderby, where the slightest wrong move can get them killed. The rulers on that world are oblivious to the subtle machinations of their underlings, one of whom has created a lookalike but false Hoya. Which one is which? And will death take the real one before March and Myrrha can stop it?

Type: Novel – science fiction

Ordering Links:
Print: https://www.hiraethsffh.com/product-page/heir-apparent-by-tyree-campbell
PDF: https://www.hiraethsffh.com/product-page/heir-apparent-by-tyree-campbell-2
ePub: https://www.hiraethsffh.com/product-page/heir-apparent-by-tyree-campbell-1

Symbiote by Amanda Bergloff

Ted
Richard E. Schell

I excitedly raced through the door as I exclaimed, "Ted, I got the technical job at the animal lab at the university." Ted, my border collie, may not understand everything I say, but that never discouraged him from sharing in my enthusiasm or disappointment. We were best of friends, and it looked like nothing would change that, especially with this new job promising to explore a groundbreaking means of gaining knowledge into the minds of our closest ally in the animal kingdom.

After adjusting to the new job, I felt I was in my element. Technicians were responsible for training dogs to tolerate the noise and distractions of having an MRI scan performed during tests. I was thrilled to be surrounded by passionate people, curious about animals and how they think. The studies promised to shed light on the workings of the animal mind.

One day at work, another animal technician told me about a home training device, a type of computerized keyboard communicator for dogs. Each key or button corresponds to a word and, when selected by one's pet, says that word out loud. She had been very impressed with her dog's progress over the first four weeks of using it. The product consisted of a colored pad for orientation to which multiple buttons were attached. The device has a wireless connection to your computer and sends your animal's real-time activity to the AI software. From there, the computer selects the next customized vocabulary settings, based on your pet's history and the information collected from all other users. From this analysis, the software optimizes your pet's learning and communication. The company stated that real-time AI analysis is applied to maximize the rate at which your pet's vocabulary skills grow, resulting in a more rewarding communication experience with your dog.

I was very enthusiastic about having a device that would allow me to open up the world of Ted's mind and provide him with a powerful tool to aid in his communication with me. The software started with selecting simple sets of words such as dinner, walk, yes, and no. It took months of dedication, but he was able to start engaging in limited communication with me using the buttons.

At first, Ted seemed to be thriving with his newfound tools for communicating and making progress every week. The software would present new buttons to master, and as his knowledge of the keyboard grew, a degree of complex reasoning seemed to emerge.

With his empowerment expanding, so did his demands. If he requested walks, I was inclined to comply with his requests to encourage his new efforts to communicate, occasionally taking an excessive amount of time that I could little afford. I grew weary with his excessive request for food and treats as well. When I would finally respond to his request with a response of "later," he persisted with the "no" and "later" response buttons repeatedly. I think I started feeling as if I was awakening to a selfish side of Ted, which I began to resent.

Likewise, Ted seemed to become increasingly more frustrated as well. It was as if he resented making requests that often were declined. From his perspective, why should he be denied extra food or time in a park, when there was a full refrigerator, and from his perspective, we had all the time in the world to spend playing?

After a time, Ted seemed to lose interest in the communicator or making requests by any means. He also seemed more distant, preferring solitude, which was out of character. I began to wonder if the AI software behind the communicator was truly effective at optimizing a pet's ability to engage with its human counterparts. At least it seemed to have failed in Ted's case.

One day upon returning home after a day at work, Ted seemed different. He was alert and took note of my entrance that day. Running straight towards me, he appeared excited at my return, something I hadn't seen in a long time. As he zoomed right past me, I realized I had left the front door open and out he ran. Chasing after him I realized I would never be able to keep up with him as he barreled down the street at full speed. Grabbing my keys, I got into the car and searched up and down every street in the neighborhood with no success.

Over the next two weeks, I searched throughout the neighborhood everywhere for him. I placed posters with his picture in storefronts, intersections and everywhere I could think of. However, months went by and as the posters deteriorated and or were lost, so too were my hopes of ever seeing Ted again. I often consider what might have happened had I just been satisfied to continue on our own as so many human-animal bondings had done in the past. Would Ted not have had the urge to suddenly leave?

There must have been a hundred times over the next two years that I would see a border collie with their characteristic black and white markings.

Each time I would wonder, could that be Ted, only to be disappointed that the markings were different or the face was not his. Each time only to be reminded of the loss of my canine friend. Emotionally I had long ago given up hope of seeing Ted again.

One day, however, I decided to take my daily walk in a different portion of the neighborhood. As I meandered down the unfamiliar street I saw a father and his two children with a border collie playing in their yard off in the distance.
As I approached the family, the closer I got to them, the more I was convinced that it was indeed Ted, enjoying an inflated ball with children as they kicked it across the yard. Suddenly aware of my presence, Ted froze and stared me straight in the eye with a look I had never seen before. His glare seemed to express both confusion and dread.
As I turned around and walked away, I realized that what I thought was a gift to Ted, was simply a mandate to meet humans on our terms. What Ted finally found was a family who was willing to communicate and connect on his.

The Man in the Chair
Mike Rader

Death stared me in the face, violent and prolonged, while I expunged every image from my film ...

My hobby has taken me to many places, but this was the first time I'd been to New Mexico. Four days driving through the desert, a yellow, red, and purple landscape of giant cliffs and groves of cottonwoods, brought me to an old, weathered sign.

It told me I was at the turnoff to a town I'd never heard of. "Tolerance." I looked around at the grim parched territory. Figured you would need a lot of tolerance to live in this wilderness.

My photographer's instincts kicked in and I swung the wheel.

The trail wasn't too unkind to my car. Soon I was surveying a dirt scrabble of a town, abandoned by the look of it. The buildings leaned in various stages of decay. A shell of an old brick building still bore the painted sign, "Tolerance Hotel." A derelict church up the road gave me a clue. Maybe this had been a town full of religious folk, some kind of sect; I heard there were lots of them out here. That vast sky encouraged thoughts of higher things.

The remains of the hotel were crying out for my camera. I slung my equipment over one shoulder and crossed to a yawning doorway. The slanting light revealed the remains of a wooden bar. Something out of a movie. I crossed the dusty timber floor toward it. My camera got to work.

I froze.

I'd heard a scraping sound from beneath my feet. I listened intently. Nothing. Then it came again, like something rubbing on metal. I'd been alone too long, I was hearing things. Time to get back to New York! But I was curious. Convinced I was the only living creature in this godforsaken town, I crossed the floor to where I saw a flight of stairs leading down into the pitch blackness.

What caught my attention was that the staircase looked modern, made of concrete. Who needed a concrete cellar in a New Mexico ghost town?

I set foot on the top step. I dug my flashlight out of my jacket and began moving down.

The cellar was cooler, the concrete walls glowing white. Reaching the bottom step, I let the flashlight beam traverse the vast space.

Suddenly it found a heavy metal door. Moving closer, I sucked in a breath.
I read the sign on the door:

ACHTUNG
HOCHFREQUENZFELD

I'd watched enough war movies to know German when I saw it. "Achtung" — a warning or a command, like "pay attention." The other words took some sorting. "Hoch" was high, I knew that. "Feld" had to be field. "High Frequency Field?"

I processed my discovery.
Why was there a German language warning —
On a bulky metal door —
In the cellar of the ruined hotel —
In the ghost town of Tolerance, New Mexico?

The more I thought about it, the more I could sense mystery — and money! With the right shots, I could deliver a unique photo essay that would guarantee sales to magazines around the world.

I paced over to the door, sensing no danger. I noted the hinges were on the outside.

I seized the handle and dragged the heavy door toward me. As it yielded, I saw it was ten inches thick. I guessed it would have to be if there was once a high frequency file behind it —

My brain sputtered.

In the center of the space, a chair contained a skeleton. Bound in place by thick leather straps. With a bizarre cap on its skull from which wires protruded.

I fired off some shots and considered my next move.

What had I found here?
A crime scene?
A torture chamber?

Cigarette butts littered the floor along with bloodstained bandages. Pliers and dental tools had been tossed to one side. Someone had worked on the poor devil in the chair.

I fired off another shot and the flash illuminated something on the far wall. A square of yellow. I moved closer. It was a photo cut from a 1930s newspaper. The face was vaguely familiar. I squinted at the remains of the caption. "J. Robert Oppenheimer."

The Oppenheimer? Had to be. I backed away, my brain racing. I struck the side of the chair and the skeleton toppled to the floor, the cap with its electrodes bouncing off the skull.

I kneeled down, studying the skull. It had a pitiful look, and I saw severe indentations on the sides and back. There was no way this could be Oppenheimer, the inventor of the atomic bomb. No way! I'd seen the movie; I knew he survived the war.

So *who* had been the man in the chair?

My heartbeats pounded in my head as I figured out the only possibility I could reach.

Fearing the consequences of Oppenheimer being kidnapped, had the FBI given him a double? Oppenheimer's work was located at Los Alamos, not that far away. So had a Nazi spy ring based itself in this ghost town, conspiring to capture the famous scientist and torture him for his secrets?

If so, the man in that chair had died a patriot.

And I carried a secret the FBI would prefer to keep buried.

Moon Bathing

by Iseult Murphy

Stood Still
Francis W. Alexander

"Hemings thought he saw a UAP," Davidson said as he and Hemings stepped past Herzog and Kline in the well-lit elevator lobby of the missile facility.

"Nah, I didn't," Javion Hemings said about the object known as an Unidentified Aerial Phenomena. "I thought the star was moving and abruptly stopped. It was a trick of the eye. Blame it on the times we're in. I'll be just fine."

"You two get it together," Herzog said before following Kline down the hall.

"Good day, gentlemen. Stay frosty," Herzog said as he stepped into the elevator.

A steady beeping sound and the sliding of the huge thick steel door reverberated throughout the room after Javion and Davidson entered. The shiny buffed floors, polished to a skating-rink-like sheen, reflected the euphoric brightness of the overhead lights. It was a stark contrast to the gloom outside, where uncertainty hung heavy.

The room's warmth blanketed Javion, a welcome shift from the bitter cold he had just left. His skin still tingled, thawing out as if he'd just awakened from hibernation. On a normal day, the faint smell of Lysol would have been refreshing, a promise of safety and order. But today, it felt like an intruder – an unwelcome reminder of Mother Earth's threats to sterilize the planet.

"Perhaps it was a supernova," Davidson said as they settled into their stations. His piercing eyes reminded Javion of Keanu Reeves, minus the facial hair.

Javion chuckled; some of the fellas said he looked like a lighter version of Denzel Washington.

"Is everything ok over there?" Davidson asked.

"I'm fine," Javion responded. He marveled at his shiny black shoes. Anxiety tried to invade his mind, but he pushed it away. He was a soldier. He looked at his blue Air Force uniform and then scratched the peach fuzz on his upper lip.

"I still have faith they will try to solve this problem," Javion said, glancing at his cross necklace—a good luck charm. This was the moment Javion Hemings hated. He realized that having all those missiles was no longer a deterrent to war. The enemy's madman had entered the realm of lunacy.

Javion felt his pulse race. At sixty feet underground, the base gave him both a secure and a claustrophobic feeling. How many lives hung in the balance above ground, he wondered. And the security guards—names he had heard of, people he knew—were now pawns in a megalomaniac's deadly game.

The phone rang, making Javion jump. He watched as Davidson answered the call.

"Objects above us?" Davidson, his face flushing a reddish hue, barked. "No one comes in here!"

Davidson hung up the phone and said, "It's a swell time to have visitors. The guards say the objects are not helicopters, planes, nor drones. So what are they?

"'I don't know,'" Davidson continued. "'I don't know sir. That's all the morons could say. That's why I don't like this woke crap. No offense, Javion."

"None taken," Javion responded. He understood that suppressed prejudices could surface in times of extreme stress.

"If the Russians hit, we will fire back!" Davidson barked.

Javion reached up and clicked the buttons that were lit on his console. He was greeted by a sound that reminded him of sheep rapidly bleating.

"Right light on number nine sir," Javion said.

"Where?" Davidson asked.

"Number nine. Warhead alarm."

"Thump the sucker," Davidson said. Sometimes, something such as a stuck button would set off the alarms.

Javion did as he was told. The red light stopped flashing and the sound stopped.

"Alarm reset," Davidson ordered.

Javion pushed two buttons on the console and reactivated the alarm. He clicked screen one and viewed the monitor. A missile appeared in its still position; wisps of smoke rose past its upturned nose. Wondering about the guards, he tapped the screen five button and viewed their stations. Although it was 9:00 at night, it looked as if the guards were under the noontime sun. Perhaps Betelgeuse had exploded.

"Sir," Javion said, "Look at screens five, six, and ten." He was thankful the light was not a flash, which would be an indication that a nuclear bomb had hit them.

Davidson looked and gasped. Five guards were highlighted as if the sun were shining on them. The women and men looked like mannequins pointing guns at the sky.

"Rodriquez," Davidson barked over the phone to the woman guard. "What's going on up there?" Javion used the camera to scan the guard. He saw Rodriquez trembling. The woman's face displayed pure horror.

"Rodriquez! What's wrong with you?" Javion shouted.

An alarm sounding like the loud chirping of mice, interrupted the men.

"Sky Eagle. This is Punt Score with a blue dash beta message in two parts." As the voice read the message, Javion got a pen and copied the code. The two men authenticated the message, opened the box on the wall, and retrieved the keys.

No, Javion thought. He broke the seal and entered the launch code.

"Launch order is confirmed," Davidson said.

The two men confirmed the orders and entered their launch keys. Like a condemned man's family yearning for the governor to pardon their loved one, Javion's Id was on standby.

"Two, one, mark."

"T minus fifty," the computerized voice said. The missiles were enabled when Javion clicked the levers.

Davidson got on the phone. "I need to hear from Washington!"

"All missiles are enabled," Javion said. Davidson responded with mumbling. Their sweat-filled faces gave them a comrade moment. That's all it gave them.

"D minus twenty-five." the computer voice said.

"I need confirmation," Davidson said.

Javion picked up the phone and listened, hoping to hear a voice say it was a mistake.

"Seven, six, five, four . . ."

"Sir, we have a launch order!" Javion said. Davidson took his hand off the key.

"Fire, sir!" Javion said. "We have our orders. The President has pressed the button!"

"We don't know that he did," Davidson answered.

Javion knew that although Davidson put on a rough face, the commander didn't want to fire the missiles either. They had to be certain that the Russians fired first. Yet, waiting too long could lead to the installation being hit with no chance for them to respond.

"Fire the missiles, sir!" Javion yelled. Beads of sweat rose from Javion's forehead as he drew his pistol and aimed it at his commander. He felt himself holding back a panic attack. What if he shot the commander and he ended up being the only man left alive? Although Javion was trained for this situation and knew he was a tough soldier, he didn't think he could handle it. Doubt was the Raven at his mind's chamber door.

He watched with relief as Davidson clicked the lever.

"Two, one, zero, one, two, three, four . . ."

"What's going on?" Javion asked. He looked at the computer screen and saw the casings fall back on the missiles.

"Thirty, thirty-one, thirty-two . . ." The panel lights blinked out

Javion reached for a key. Suddenly, he could not move. This moment reminded him of the sleep paralysis he had as a child. Only his eyes could move. He spotted Davidson trembling. He heard mumbling, a chorus between himself and the commander.

Javion's Adams Apple threatened to plunge into his stomach. He sensed that some "thing" was in the room with them which now placed him in night terror mode. His mouth hung open as he stared

wide-eyed at a grey, peach-headed alien standing between him and the commander.
Where did that being come from? he thought.
The alien blinked its black oval eyes. Then it disappeared.

Javion felt something on his right shoulder. In his peripheral field of vision, he saw three bony fingers moving close to his neck. The tremens were having a field day with him. He needed to relieve himself. Although Davidson was in the room with him, he felt alone and helpless. He resembled a paralyzed fly ensnared in a spider's web, its chelicerae clashing, as the spider spun it.

He closed his eyes. Suddenly, he felt calm. The fingers turned out to be quite soothing.

Right when he began to feel comfortable, the fingers went away. He was able to move.

The computers and lights abruptly shut off stunning him. Javion reached for the Maglite under his seat.

The lights returned, making him jump and drop the flashlight clattering onto the floor. As he retrieved the tool, the phone rang. Javion watched Davidson answer it.

"I don't know sir," Davidson said. Javion walked over to listen to the conversation.

"The President is talking to their leader now," the person on the other end of the phone said.

Javion watched as the life returned to his panel with lights flashing greens, blues, reds, and yellows.

"What happened?" Javion shouted.

"Maybe a solar storm," the person on the line said.

"Get ready," the person continued, "in case we have to fire the missiles."

Fit for a Queen
Pamela Love

Glory Leonard, youngest ever Nobel Prizewinner for chemistry, hands me her invitation to this year's Earth Fashion Expo. "I'm ready for the scanner," she says, a challenge in her voice.

I'm Director of Security here at the Lake Tanganyika Conference Center. With all these VIPs, I'm the one operating the sensor gates, which I gesture toward courteously—but only after doublechecking my earplugs. If the scanner detects fur or feathers, its blare causes people nearby to lose control of certain bodily functions—a powerful incentive to obey Tanzania's law against wearing them. Nevertheless, over her elegant black gown, Doctor Leonard flaunts a golden cloak which certainly *seems* to be fur. *Fit for a queen,* I think. A lioness? No, she wouldn't dare.

Yet there is something about her knowing smile that suggests she would indeed. At the sight of her, the crowd of world-famous models, designers, manufacturers, and media retreat. Smirking, she waits until they have put a good fifteen meters' distance between themselves and imminent cacophony. Everyone holds their breath and ears, except her.

She seems to float through the gate—which remains silent as she passes. A roar of admiration pours from almost every throat, followed by the question, "How?"

Leonard's answer? A mysterious smile, one that makes the Mona Lisa's look like a grin.

So the guesswork begins. A writer who was issuing opinions on fashion before Doctor Leonard's birth gives a snort. "Fake fur, though I must admit it's the best I've ever seen."

"What it is, is authentic." The Nobelist runs a hand across the magnificent garment. She holds out a fold, and at her urging, some audience members touch it.

"Sure feels like hair. *Human* hair—got to be. That won't set off the scanner, or anyone entering the Expo would have to be bald," one model calls out. Leonard shakes her head.

"Such a beautiful shade of gold . . . *could* it be gold? Some ultra-flexible alloy, perhaps?" asks a designer.

"Wrong again." The scientist twirls, her cloak rippling like a field of teff in the wind. "I created this in my lab."

Leonard even beckons to me. Yes, she's confident enough to let me examine the cloak. As my fingertips brush through the hair, my gut twists. I'd bet my bank account something living once wore that . . . that *pelt*.

Could it be grown from some kind of cells scraped from a lion? Maybe one in captivity? I almost suggest it, before turning away, silent. The scanner would have detected that.

Then I suck in my breath. Has she developed some kind of chemical that masks fur so a scanner can't detect it? She *is* a world-class chemist. Here, she can find a market. Fur may come back into fashion if scanners can't keep it out. That means danger, not just for lions, but leopards, cheetahs, and countless other mammals all over the world. They're so close to extinction already.

My comm link buzzes. "Director Juma, our monitors are picking up what seems like multiple drones. They do not have clearance to approach."

"Go to alert status two. Heighten the scans. Keep me informed." My pulse speeds up. Until now, a terrorist attack had been my greatest worry about the EFE.

A guard dashes to my side. "Should we evacuate?"

"No. Any danger is outside. All entry points are locked. The guests are safer here."

A famous merchandiser points to the windows. "What's that? Look!"

A dark, seething mass covers the glass, blocking out all natural light. There's a not-quite stampede as people scramble away from this threat. They huddle in the middle of the hall.

I raise my hand. "Remain calm. Those are microbots. We will deal with them." I whisper a code into my comm link. In moments an electromagnetic pulse will disable the tiny drones outside, sending them rattling to the ground like hail. The building itself is shielded.

Minutes pass. If anything, the microbots' activity accelerates. Their number is definitely increasing.

Wonderful. Doctor Leonard has invented something to screen fur against sensors. Has someone else invented something to screen drones against an EM pulse? Quite a coincidence, that. Stepping toward the window, I squint. Microbots often resemble insects, but these drones look very lifelike . . .

"Doctor Leonard?" Now it's my turn to call her over. Defiant, she strides up to me. I whisper, "I'm about to call for a smoke bomb to handle what's outside. Will you confirm that's the right thing to do?"

She folds her arms. "You're the security expert."

"And you're the genius who made a cloak out of queen honeybees."

Her lips tighten. "Hair grown from their cells, yes. Your scanners aren't calibrated for that. What I've done is legal."

"I doubt that swarm cares. Listen. Maybe your process increases pheromones somehow? I'm no expert, but they sound much more aggressive than usual. Smoke will tranquilize them."

As I lift my comm link, Doctor Leonard is looking at the crowd. Some people are sobbing. Some pray. Many are trying desperately to place calls. "Wait. I have a better idea."

My eyebrows lift when she explains. "You're sure?"

Without another word, she heads to the elevator.

Moments later, Doctor Leonard opens a fourth-story window. She flings out the golden cloak, which billows as it falls. Instantly, the swarm speeds through the air, settling on top of it when it hits the ground.

It doesn't take long for someone to figure out the cloak's secret through the now-clear glass. "Bug fur?" shrieks one manufacturer. "From killer bees?" When Glory Leonard steps out of the elevator, she is met with a round of boos.

Not from me, however. "Thank you, Doctor." I sweep her my finest bow, one fit for a queen.

Author and Artist Bios

Francis Wesley Alexander is the author of *When the Mushrooms Come* (Hiraeth). His stories have been published in *Hungur Chronicles, Alien Dimensions, Night to Dawn, Spaceships & Spidersilk, Outposts of the Beyond, Tales from the Moonlit Path, Creative Brother,* and *Residential Aliens.*

James Aitchison is an Australian author of more than 200 books. Writing short fiction as Mike Rader, his work has appeared in many leading publications and online journals. Writing as James Lee, his horror stories for middle readers in Asia inspired the Netflix series, *Mr Midnight: Beware the Monsters.*

Amanda Bergloff is a digital/mixed media artist of the weirder things in life. Her cover art has been published by the Jules Verne Society's *Extraordinary Visions Anthology, Utopia Science Fiction, Fear Forge, The Horror Zine,* and others. She lives in Denver, Colorado and is a shameless collector of over 4,000 horror paperbacks, along with vintage toys and comics. Follow her on X @AmandaBergloff

Stephen W. Chappell is the chosen servant of four feline overlords, who tolerate his service in the outskirts of the NJ pine barrens. He is currently working as a systems engineer. Besides writing, he enjoys making photographs and reading.

Paul Lonardo is a freelance writer and author of both fiction and nonfiction books who has placed numerous short stories and nonfiction articles in a variety of horror/dark fantasy magazines and ezines. He is a contributing writer for several publications, including *Tales from the Moonlit Path*. He is an active HWA member. Visit Paul's author website: www.thegoblinpitcher.com
Instagram: @PaulLonardo13
X: @PaulLonardo

Pamela Love was born in New Jersey. After graduating from Bucknell University and working as a teacher and in marketing, she turned to writing. Her speculative fiction has (or will soon) appear in *Flash Digest, Spaceports and Spidersilk, Tales from the Moonlit Path, Luna Station Quarterly, Space Squid,* and *Havok: Animal Kingdom,* among other publications. She lives in Maryland.

Iseult Murphy loves to tell stories, whether it is through pencils and chalk on paper or written words in a book. She combines her love of animals and nature with her dark and magical imagination to produce artwork in different media. Find out more at iseultmurphy.com.

Richard E. Schell works in the biomedical field in California. He enjoys writing and has published over 100 articles and other works in both the biomedical field as well as in fictional genres and poetry. He enjoys photography, literature and travel. He also volunteers in animal rescue.

TRANSMISSION ENDS

www.ingramcontent.com/pod-product-compliance
Lightning Source LLC
LaVergne TN
LVHW021953060526
838201LV00049B/1688